W9-BFI-628

And the Winner Is...

by Jenny Miglis   illustrated by Caleb Meurer

Based on the teleplay *Big Pink Loser* by Jay Lender,
William Reiss, and Merriwether Williams

SCHOLASTIC INC.

New York   Toronto   London   Auckland   Sydney
Mexico City   New Delhi   Hong Kong   Buenos Aires

Based on the TV series *SpongeBob SquarePants*® created by Stephen Hillenburg as seen on Nickelodeon®

ISBN 0-439-59888-5

12 11 10 9 8 7 6 5 4 3 2 1   4 5 6 7 8 9/0

Printed in the U.S.A.

First Scholastic printing, April 2004

One morning Patrick received a package in the mail. It was a trophy! He could barely contain his excitement. "My very first award!" he cried with glee. "I've got to show SpongeBob!"

Patrick barreled through SpongeBob's front door. He cleared his throat and read aloud, "'For Outstanding Achievement in Achievement . . . SpongeBob SquarePants?' Huh? That's a funny way to spell my name!"

SpongeBob looked down at his feet. "Uh, Patrick, there must be some mistake," he said. "That award is for me."

"B-b-but I never won an award before," Patrick whined. "It's so shiny."
"I've got something else that's shiny in my coat closet! A button!"
said SpongeBob. "You can have it!"

"Goody! I'll get it!" Patrick cried. He flung open the door of a nearby closet. Awards and trophies of all shapes and sizes tumbled out.

"Not there!" SpongeBob cried. "That's my . . . award closet," he mumbled.

CRASH!

"Waah! I want an award!" Patrick wailed. "I'm not good at anything!"

SpongeBob wrapped his arm around Patrick's shoulder. "But you're Patrick STAR!" he exclaimed. "You can do anything you set your mind to!"

"Okay, I want to defeat the giant monkey men and save the ninth dimension!" Patrick said.

"That's too big. Something smaller," SpongeBob said.

"Defeat the little monkey men and save the eighth dimension?" Patrick asked.

SpongeBob sighed. "The smallest thing you can think of!" he said.

Patrick thought for a moment. "A job at the Krusty Krab?"

"Great idea!" said SpongeBob. "Let's go!"

"It was nice of Mr. Krabs to give me a job here. Do I get my award yet?" Patrick asked as he ate a Krabby Patty.

"You have to work for it," SpongeBob said, reminding him. "Pick up this order and take it to the customers," he instructed.

Patrick picked up the food and walked toward the table in the back. But just as he reached it he tripped, spilling Krabby Patties all over the floor.

"Good try," SpongeBob said. "But next time make sure the food actually gets to the customer."

"Why don't you answer the phone?" SpongeBob suggested.

"Aye, aye, captain!" Patrick exclaimed as the first call rang in.

"Is this the Krusty Krab?" the customer on the line asked.

"No, this is Patrick," Patrick replied and hung up.

The phone rang again. *Briiing! Briiing!*
"Hello, is this the Krusty Krab?" the second customer asked.

"NO! This is PATRICK!" Patrick hollered. "And I am NOT a crusty crab!"
SpongeBob shook his head. "That's the name of the restaurant, Patrick."
"Aww, fishpaste," Patrick said with a sigh. "I can't do anything right."

"Sure you can, Patrick," SpongeBob encouraged. "Uh, you can . . . you're good at . . . hmm . . ." He couldn't think of anything. "I've got it! I bet you know how to open a jar!"

SpongeBob took a jar of tartar sauce from the shelf and unscrewed the lid. "It's easy! Now you try. First, get a jar," he instructed.

Patrick rooted around in the refrigerator and emerged holding something that was clearly not a jar.

"No, Patrick, that's a pickle," SpongeBob said patiently.

After a few tries Patrick finally found a jar of jellyfish jelly.

"Good. Now just do exactly as I do. Exactly," said SpongeBob as he demonstrated.

"Exactly," Patrick repeated as he slowly turned the lid until it popped off.

"Oh, no! I broke it!" Patrick cried.

"No, Patrick, you did it!" SpongeBob exclaimed. "Good job!"

"I did?" Patrick asked with disbelief. "I opened the jar with my own hand! And it was all because you showed me how to do it, SpongeBob!"

"Patrick, if you do exactly what I do you'll have an award in no time!"

The next day Patrick greeted SpongeBob outside his house.

"Wow!" SpongeBob said. "It's amazing how a simple change of clothes can make a guy look just like . . . me!" He did a double take. "Huh?"

Patrick straightened his tie. "If I'm going to be a winner, I've got to dress like one," he declared.

"Okay, Patrick, whatever you say," SpongeBob said with a shrug. "Are you ready for work? I'm ready!"

"I'm ready! I'm ready! I'm ready!" Patrick chanted.

"Oops! Forgot my hat!" SpongeBob said.

"Oops! Me too!" Patrick said.

"Come on," SpongeBob said. "Back to the old grind."

"Come on, back to the old grind," Patrick repeated.

"Why are you copying me?" he asked Patrick.

"Why are you copying me?" Patrick repeated. "I want to win awards just like you, SpongeBob."

"Well, it's annoying, so stop it!" SpongeBob cried.

Patrick shrugged his shoulders. "Stop it," he mumbled under his breath

"Aaaaaagh!" SpongeBob screamed. Then he had an idea. "Hi! My name is Patrick Star!" he said. "I'm the laziest, pinkest starfish in Bikini Bottom and I wish I were ME and not SpongeBob!"

But this time Patrick didn't imitate SpongeBob. "What's so great about being a big pink nobody? I was never closer to an award than the minute I started copying you," he said and hung his head.

Just then a delivery truck pulled up.
"Trophy delivery!" the truck driver called out.
"Must be another award for SpongeBob
TrophyPants!" Patrick sneered. "What's it for this
time, perfect squareness?"

SpongeBob took the trophy and held it up to the light. "'For Doing Absolutely Nothing Longer Than Anyone Else,'" he read, "'Patrick Star.'" SpongeBob couldn't believe his eyes. "Patrick! This trophy is for you!"

"For me?" Patrick gasped. "I always knew I'd win an award!"

"So, what are you going to do now that you've won it?" SpongeBob asked. Patrick propped himself up against the trophy. "Nothing, of course," Patrick said. "I've got to protect my title!"